AHCHOO!
LION'S GOT THE FLU

Written and Illustrated by Hagino Chinatsu

PURPLE BEAR BOOKS · NEW YORK

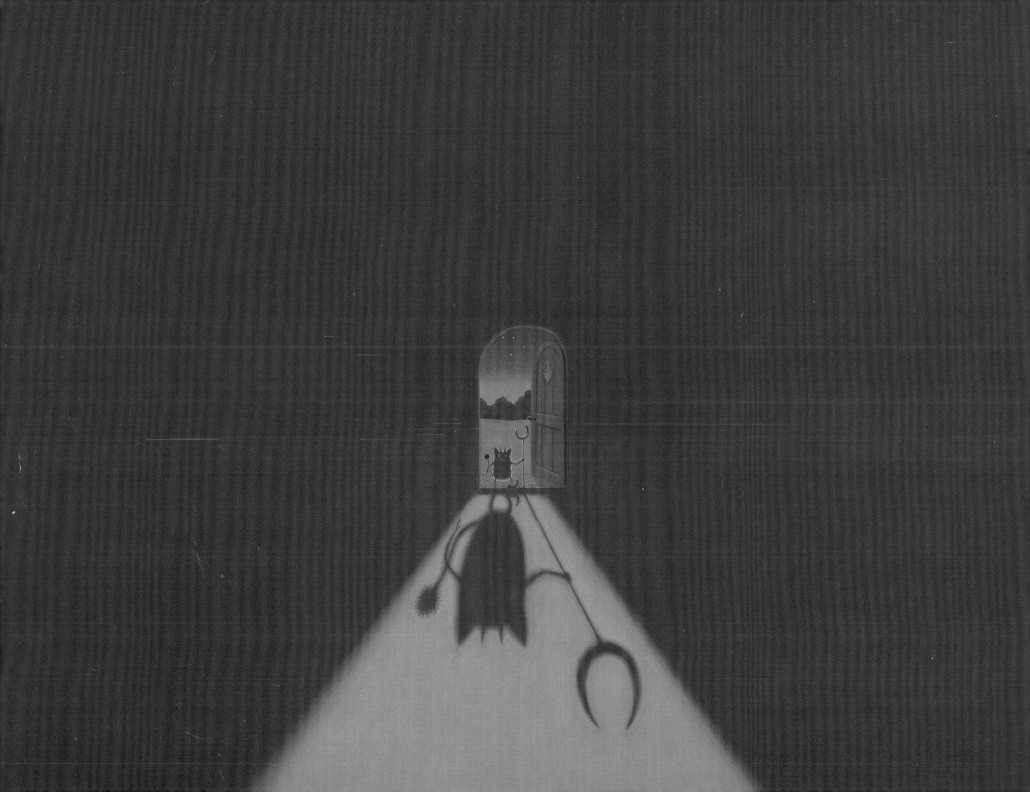

Lion was sick. He'd caught a flu bug.
He had a sore throat and a fever and ached all over.

So Lion stayed in bed, resting quietly, until . . .

Knock! Knock!

Someone was at the door.

Ahchoo! sneezed Lion. "Come in, please."

The Mouse Brothers tiptoed in, carrying a big cake.
"We heard you were sick," they said, "so we baked you
a cake to cheer you up."
Ahchoo! sneezed Lion. "Thank you very much."
Knock! Knock! Someone else was at the door.

Cat and Rabbit scurried in.

"How are you feeling?" asked Rabbit. "Here, have some delicious carrots. They'll help you get well soon."

"And here's some ice cream," said Cat. "It will help, too."

Ahchoo! sneezed Lion. He thanked his friends politely, even though he wasn't sure the carrots and ice cream would really help.

Knock! Knock! Now who was it?

Elephant lumbered in.

"Here are some bananas," he said. "They'll make you as strong as I am."

Ahchoo! sneezed Lion. "Oh, thanks . . . I'll save them for later."

Knock! Knock!

In came Aardvark.

"Cheer up, Lion," he said. "Here's a nest full of yummy ants!"

Ahchoo! sneezed Lion. "That's so thoughtful of you. But could you please take the ants outside?"

Knock! Knock!

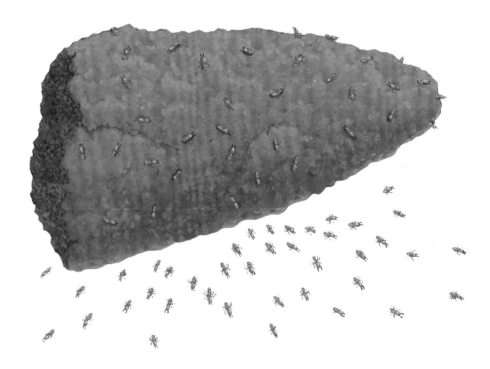

Bear poked his head in the door.
"Hi, Lion!" he said. "Look what I have for you!
This beehive is filled with sweet honey."

Ouch! yelled Lion as a bee
stung him on the nose.
"That *is* a sweet gift," he said,
"but could you please put it
outside for now?"
Knock! Knock!

Fox opened the door and bowed.

"Hello there, Lion," he said. "I have a big surprise for you."

Fox tapped his wand on his top hat and out popped . . .

. . . a fierce-looking dragon waving a get-well flag!
Everyone shrieked in surprise.
More animals came in to see what was happening.

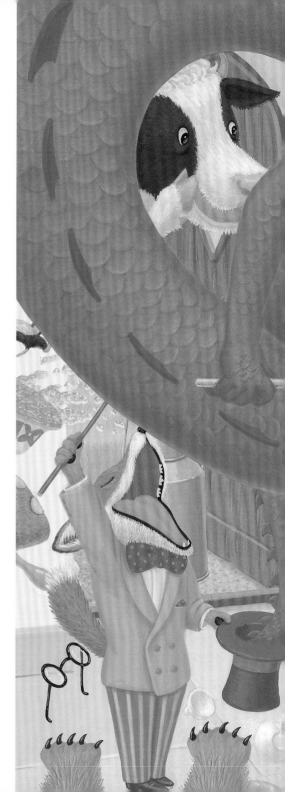

Knock! Knock!

Hippopotamus, Alligator, and the Pig Sisters arrived.
"You must be bored, just lying in bed," they said. "So we're going to put on a show for you."

Hippopotamus played the drums, the Pig Sisters danced and
shook their tambourines, and Alligator performed a high-wire act.
Everyone clapped and cheered.
Everyone, that is, except for Lion.
"Oooh, how my head aches!" he moaned.
Then through the door came . . .

. . . the Raccoon Family.

"Let's start a fire to keep you toasty warm," they said.

Ahchoo! sneezed Lion. "No! No fire, please!"

CRASH!
Through the window flew the witch who lived in the forest.
"Never fear, my magic's here!" she declared. "Abracadabra,
turn off the heat, water will get you back on your feet."
She waved her wand and . . .

. . . rain poured down from the ceiling, drenching everything.

Lion had had enough.
"Oooh! I feel worse than ever!"
he moaned.

Then he scrunched up his eyes, wrinkled his nose, and *ah* . . .

ah . . .

ah . . .

AHCHOOOOOOO!

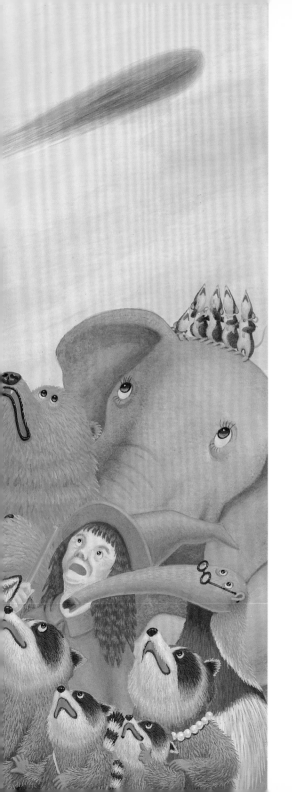

Lion let out a tremendous sneeze that shook the whole house and sent something flying out of his mouth.

It was the flu bug!

"Sorry I made you sick," he said sheepishly.

"That's alright," said Lion. "Now that you're out I'm feeling much better."

That evening all of them threw a big party.
They sang and danced around the campfire, feasted on cake, carrots, ice cream, and bananas, and drank tea with sweet honey.
Lion and his friends had a wonderful time—and the flu bug did, too!

Translated by Annie Kung

Copyright © 2005 by Hagino Chinatsu

English translation copyright © 2006 by Purple Bear Books Inc.

First published in Taiwan in 2005 by Grimm Press

First English-language edition published in 2006 by Purple Bear Books Inc., New York.

For more information about our books, visit our website: purplebearbooks.com

Library of Congress Cataloging-in-Publication Data is available.

This edition prepared by Cheshire Studio.

Trade edition
ISBN-10: 1-933327-26-X
ISBN-13: 978-1-933327-26-6
10 9 8 7 6 5 4 3 2 1

Library edition
ISBN-10: 1-933327-27-8
ISBN-13: 978-1-933327-27-3
10 9 8 7 6 5 4 3 2 1

Printed in Taiwan